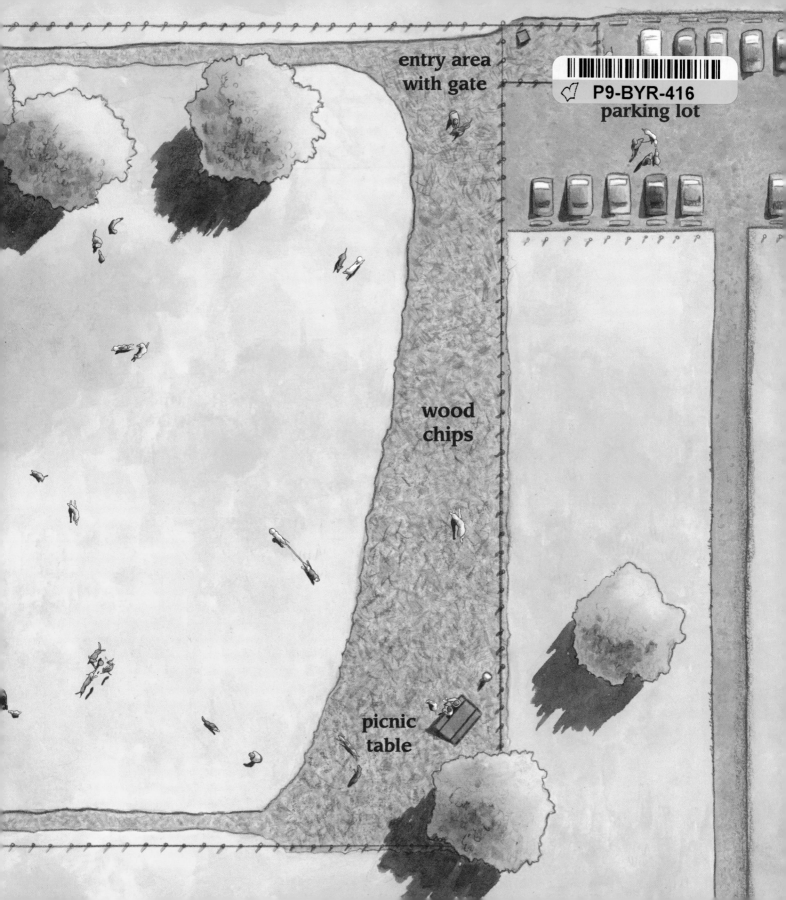

entry area
with gate

parking lot

wood
chips

picnic
table

The Gryphon Press
—a voice for the voiceless—

**This book is dedicated
to dog lovers everywhere,
with special thanks
to those who have made dog parks a reality
across the United States, and in other parts of the world.**

Design by Rachel Holscher
Text set in Leawood by Prism Publication Services
Manufactured in Canada by Friesens Corporation

Library of Congress Control Number: 2006923846

ISBN-10: 0-940719-00-2
ISBN-13: 978-0-940719-00-2

1 3 5 7 9 10 8 6 4 2

A portion of profits from this book will be
donated to shelters and animal rescue societies.

---

*I am the voice of the voiceless:
Through me, the dumb shall speak;
Till the deaf world's ear be made to hear
The cry of the wordless weak.*
—from a poem by Ella Wheeler Wilcox, early 20th-century poet

At The Dog Park

with
Sam and Lucy

Daisy Bix • **Amelia Hansen**

The Gryphon Press
—a voice for the voiceless—

Almost there!

Almost there!

Please hurry.

At last!

I'm free!

Let's go!

My person likes it here. • Yes, mine, too.

Play? • Okay.

Hey, up there, what's new? • I'm thinking.

Where have you been? • Great mud.

Mine! • No, mine!

I'm right behind you!

Wow! • I'll get it!

I'm way ahead. • No, you're not.

You're new here. • I really like you.

Is that your person? • Sure is. • I have a new collar.

Hello there. • Nice to meet you.

I've got it! • My Frisbee! • No, I've got it!

Hey! • I see you. • Can't get me! • Or me!

Are they fighting? • No, just playing.

That was great! See you soon.   •   Yes, that *was* great. See you soon!

Maybe tomorrow . . . we'll go again.

Running . . . sniffing . . . fun . . . friends . . .

A Dog Park is a safe, fenced place where non-aggressive dogs and puppies can be off leash. Some dog parks are small, with a few trees. Others enclose acres of trails and woodland with a pond or a stream. Each dog park has its own character, but most have a fence with a double-gated entry, parking, shaded areas, a place to dispense plastic bags, and trash cans where owners dispose of their dog's wastes.

A Dog Park Is Good for Dogs and People because it promotes responsible pet ownership. Dogs who run and play work off their boundless energy. An exercised off-leash dog is friendly toward people and other animals, meeting other dogs in a safe, neutral place. A dog park encourages people to be outdoors. It's also a place to meet other dog lovers. A dog park provides the elderly and owners with disabilities an accessible place to exercise their canine companions.

The Rules at Most Dog Parks are about safety and health, including keeping the park waste free. These rules usually apply: • All dogs must be currently licensed. • Puppies and adult dogs must be in good health with proper inoculations, as well as being parasite free, internally and externally. • Dogs must be on leash until they are completely inside the enclosed area and put back on leash before exiting the enclosed area. • No dog displaying aggressive behavior toward other dogs or people is allowed. (The dog park is intended for fun and play—not to be a dangerous place.) • Owners must clean up after their dogs. • Owners must never leave their dogs unattended and must monitor the activity of their dogs. • Parents or guardians must look after their children at all times; young children should play only with their own dog and be closely supervised.

For a Good Experience at the Dog Park, let your dog take the initiative and pay attention to his/her responses. If the dog appears anxious or frightened, leash up and come back another time. Stay with your dog. Always make sure your dog is in your sight. If you have a rescue dog, remember that his past experience with other dogs may not have been happy. It takes time to heal a broken spirit and to build trust. Always use positive training techniques, not harsh ones. For a puppy to have a good experience, wait until it is four months old before you visit, and, the first few times, try to go on weekday mornings or early afternoons when the park is not too busy.

Starting a Dog Park in Your Community will take a few like-minded people working together to convince your town or city planning commission that a dog park, like other community recreational facilities, is not only a legitimate recreational use for public land but an excellent use of community funding. There is detailed advice on the process of starting a dog park at many online resources, such as:

The Bark at http://www.thebark.com/community/advocacy_dogParks/dogParks.html
dogpark.com at http://www.dogpark.com/index.php?id=12,0,0,1,0,0
Dog Play at http://www.dog-play.com/dogpark.html#how

fence

pond

path